Augusto y su sonrisa

Augustus and his Smile

Mantra Lingua
303 Ballards Lane, London N12 8NP
www.mantralingua.com

First published in UK
by Little Tiger Press 2006
This edition published 2012

Audio copyright ©
Mantra Lingua 2008

Thank you, Mum, Brian and Colin - C R

Augusto y su sonrisa

Augustus and his Smile

Catherine Rayner

Spanish translation by
Marta Belen Saez-Cabero

Mantra Lingua

El tigre Augusto estaba triste.
Había perdido su sonrisa.

Augustus the tiger was sad.
He had lost his smile.

Así que se dio un estirón tigresco ENORME
y partió en su búsqueda.

So he did a HUGE tigery stretch and set off to find it.

Primero se deslizó bajo una mata de arbustos. Halló un pequeño escarabajo brillante, pero no encontró su sonrisa.

First he crept under a cluster of bushes. He found a small, shiny beetle, but he couldn't see his smile.

Then he climbed to the tops of the tallest trees.
He found birds that chirped and called,
but he couldn't find his smile.

Después trepó a las copas de los árboles más altos.
Halló pájaros gorjeando y cantando,
pero no encontró su sonrisa.

Augusto buscó y buscó, cada vez más lejos.
Escaló las cumbres de las montañas más altas donde nubes que
anunciaban nieve se arremolinaban creando dibujos de
escarcha en el aire glacial.

Further and further Augustus searched.
He scaled the crests of the highest mountains where the snow
clouds swirled, making frost patterns in the freezing air.

Buceó hasta el fondo de los océanos más profundos y
jugó y chapoteó con bancos de diminutos peces brillantes.

He swam to the bottom of the deepest oceans and
splished and splashed with shoals of tiny, shiny fish.

Hizo cabriolas y se paseó por el más grande de los desiertos,
haciendo sombras de diferentes formas bajo el sol.
Augusto caminó más
y más lejos
a través de arenas movedizas
hasta que …

He pranced and paraded through
the largest desert, making
shadow shapes in the sun.
Augustus padded further
and further
through shifting sand
until …

... pitter patter

pitter patter

drip

drop

plop!

… plic ploc

plic ploc

plic

ploc

¡plaf!

Augusto bailó
y corrió
mientras las gotas de lluvia rebotaban
y volaban.

Augustus danced
and raced
as raindrops bounced
and flew.

Chapoteó en los charcos, cada vez más grandes y profundos.
Se abalanzó hacia un enorme charco azul plateado
y vio …

He splashed through puddles, bigger and deeper.
He raced towards a huge silver-blue puddle
and saw …

...justo bajo su hocico
... ¡su sonrisa!

... there under his nose
... his smile!

Y Augusto se dio cuenta de que su sonrisa estaría ahí,
siempre que él fuera feliz.

Tan sólo tenía que nadar con los peces o bailar en los charcos,
o escalar las montañas y mirar el mundo – ya que la felicidad
estaría siempre a su alrededor.

Augusto estaba tan feliz que se puso a saltar

y a brincar …

And Augustus realized that his smile would be there,
whenever he was happy.

He only had to swim with the fish or dance in the puddles,
or climb the mountains and look at the world – for happiness
was everywhere around him.

Augustus was so pleased that
he hopped
and skipped …

... y se fue dando saltos y
sonriendo.

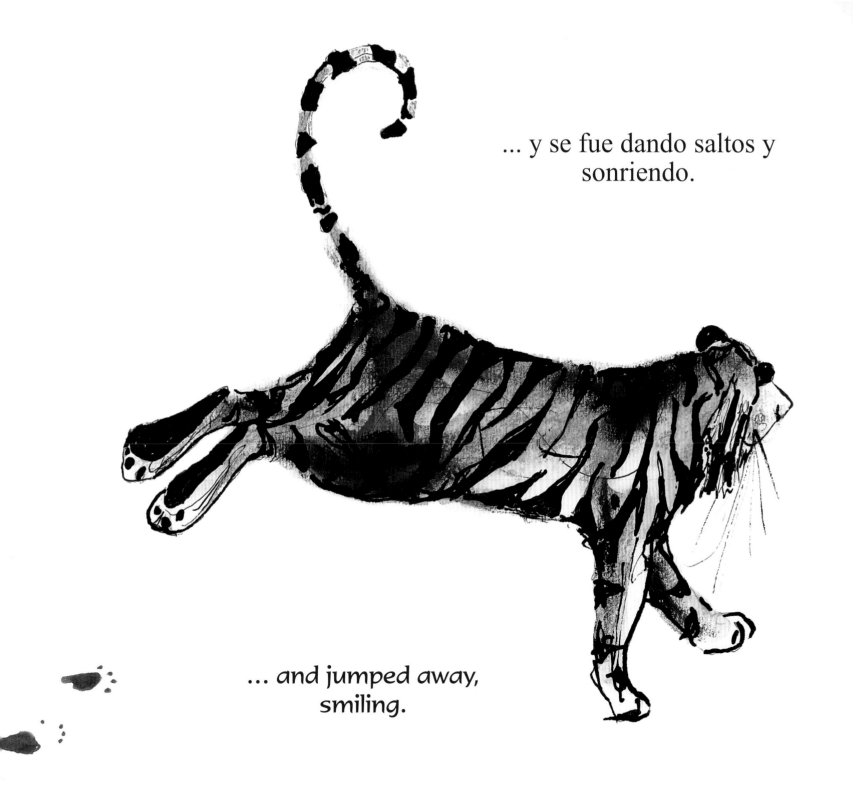

... and jumped away,
smiling.

Amazing tiger facts

Augustus is a Siberian tiger.

Siberian tigers are the biggest cats in the world!
They live in Southern Russia and Northern China
where the winters are very cold.

Most tigers are orange with black stripes.
The stripes make them hard to see when they
walk through tall weeds and grasses.

Tigers are good swimmers and like to cool down
by sitting in waterholes.

Each tiger's stripes are different to those of
other tigers – like a human finger print.

Tigers are in danger ...

Tigers are only hunted by one animal ... HUMANS!
And humans are ruining the land on which tigers live.

There are more tigers living in zoos and nature reserves than
in the wild. There are only about 6000 tigers left in the wild.

Help save the tiger!

World Wildlife Fund (WWF)
Panda House
Weyside Park
Godalming
Surrey GU7 1XR
Tel: 01483 426 444
www.wwf.org.uk

David Shepherd Wildlife
Foundation
61 Smithbrook Kilns
Cranleigh
Surrey GU76 8JJ
Tel: 01483 727 323/267 924
www.davidshepherd.org